Princess Betony
AND THE UNICORN

First published in 2012
by Walker Books Australia Pty Ltd
Locked Bag 22, Newtown
NSW 2042 Australia
www.walkerbooks.com.au

This edition published in 2016.

The moral rights of the author and illustrator have been asserted.

National Library of Australia Cataloguing-in-Publication entry:
Freeman, Pamela, 1960– author.
Princess Betony and the unicorn / Pamela Freeman; illustrator: Tamsin Ainslie.
ISBN: 978 1 925381 02 3 (paperback)
Series: Freeman, Pamela, 1960– Princess Betony; 1.
For children.
Subjects: Unicorns – Juvenile fiction.
          Children's stories.
Other Creators/Contributors: Ainslie, Tamsin, 1974– illustrator.
A823.3

The illustrations for this book were created with
pencil and watercolour paint
Typeset in Garamond
Printed and bound in China

Princess Betony
AND THE UNICORN

Pamela Freeman

⊰ ILLUSTRATED BY TAMSIN AINSLIE ⊱

WALKER BOOKS
AND SUBSIDIARIES

LONDON • BOSTON • SYDNEY • AUCKLAND

↤ CHAPTER ONE ↦

Princess Betony curled up tight underneath the desk in the Royal Library of Floramonde and held the book she had been reading close, her finger crammed between the pages to keep her place. The book wriggled in her grasp, its pages rustling.

"Shh," Betony whispered to it. It stopped struggling, but the pages flicked back and forth against her hands, tickling. Betony wanted to laugh, but she didn't dare.

She could hear Lady Pineal's heels tapping on the marble tiles of the corridor and then – nothing. Had she gone? Or were her footsteps muffled by the thick library carpet?

"Princess Betony, where *are* you?" Lady Pineal half-sang, which was her way of shouting, because a lady never shouts.

Betony tried hard not to breathe. If she buried her head in her arms and scrunched up smaller, maybe …

"There you are!" Lady Pineal said, exasperated. Her skinny hand reached under the desk and pulled Betony out. "What do you have there?"

Lady Pineal was Betony's governess, and chose all the books Betony read. Reluctantly, Betony gave her the book, although it tried to cling to Betony's small fingers. Lady Pineal gasped, holding one hand dramatically to her heart to show how shocked she was.

You might have thought, looking at her face, that it was a rude book, or a dangerous book, or a too-old book, but it wasn't. It was a book of fairytales.

"Your Highness, you know you are not allowed to read the books in this section of the library," Lady Pineal started, in that tone of "what am I going to do with you?" which Betony hated the most.

"Well?" Lady Pineal demanded. "What do you have to say for yourself?"

She was waiting for Betony to say "sorry", as a well brought up young princess should. But Betony didn't want to say she was sorry. She *wasn't* sorry. She didn't understand why she couldn't read fairytales. They were wonderful stories, all about magic and wizards and dragons and princesses too – although she had to admit that the princesses in them were mostly rather silly and always needed somebody to rescue them.

As if agreeing with Betony, the book leaped out of Lady Pineal's hands. It flew up into the air, opened wide, and then snapped itself shut on the end of Lady Pineal's very long nose. She yelped. Betony tried hard not to laugh.

The book made a noise very like a chuckle and flew back to the shelf where Betony had found it.

"You see?" Lady Pineal demanded, rubbing her red nose. "You *see*?" To herself, she said, "King Max really needs a wizard to keep these books in order."

Princess Betony knew that wizards existed in Floramonde, that magic happened all over the country, but the flying book was the most magical thing she had ever seen. Lady Pineal had never even said the *word* "wizard" to her before, and she refused to let Betony have anything to do with anything magical or interesting. Even fairytales.

"I would like to read that book, Lady Pineal," Princess Betony said. The book had given her courage. "Please." And as Lady Pineal took in a deep breath, ready to scold again, she added, "My mother would let me, I think."

Lady Pineal's eyes flashed and she muttered, "Of course *she* would–" And then she closed her mouth tight and went red, as though she was about to say something unladylike. Betony knew what it was though – something like: "Of course *she* would – your mother is a tree!"

"Your mother," Lady Pineal said, after

a long pause, "is not in charge of your education. *I* am. Your father has agreed to this, as you very well know."

Now maybe Betony would have argued some more, or maybe she wouldn't have, but at that moment a laugh came from the next room.

Her mother's laugh, silvery and delighted.

⊰ CHAPTER TWO ⊱

Betony slipped past Lady Pineal and ran to her mother's chamber. Perhaps her mother could *order* Lady Pineal to let her read the book. She was the queen, after all.

The queen's chamber was the room where she read and did paperwork. It was a lot like the king's chamber in size and shape, with high vaulted ceilings and tall windows overlooking the palace gardens. Only yesterday it had looked a lot like Betony's father's chamber, too: full of books and maps and work tables. Entirely human.

But today – Betony stopped on the

threshold, eyes wide. Today her mother's chamber was like a forest. There were pots set at every corner and, out of those pots, plants were growing. Vines and ferns and flowering bushes, even a couple of tiny maple trees, which shot up and grew taller even as she watched. Magic! she thought. At last, I'm getting to see real magic!

All over the room the green shoots from the plants were reaching out, reaching up, climbing the walls and across the high ceilings, threading around the curtain rods and over the bookshelves. The room *rustled*, the shoots were growing so fast.

In the middle of the room were her mother and the Chief Palace Gardener, Rosie. They were smiling. Queen Salixia was tall and slender, dressed always in green. Today she was in spring green, a colour so light it was almost golden, and she had left her long, yellow hair loose. Here, in her own chamber, she went barefoot and without her crown.

Betony thought her mother looked just like the willow tree dryad that she had once been.

Betony sighed. She wished she were magical too. But as far as she could tell, she was just plain human, with no dryad in her at all.

Now you have probably never met a dryad. Dryads are tree people. There are as many kinds of dryads as there are trees, and the dryads live inside the trees like your mind lives inside your head – except that dryads can step out of the tree and then they look like real people. Betony's mother had been a dryad whose tree was killed by a storm, but Betony's father, Max, had loved her so much that somehow she hadn't died, even though a dryad without a tree *always* dies. She had come back to the palace with him instead and become queen.

You would think with a mother as magical as Salixia, in a place as magical as Floramonde, that Betony's life would be full of enchantment. But it wasn't because the Royal Council didn't approve. They were glad Betony was just human, plain and reliable. The Royal Council liked things to be predictable. Magic wasn't predictable at all. So they kept Betony right away from anything that wasn't human, just in case she turned out to be magical also.

The queen looked around as Betony came into the chamber and she held out her arms. Betony ran into them for a hug.

"What do you think of my grove?" her mother asked.

Betony looked around, feeling a delicious tingle work its way through her, from the ends of her toes to the tips of her fingers. She felt as though her hair was trying to grow as fast as the vines climbing up the walls. This was the first time she had ever seen her mother do anything a human couldn't do. It made her wonder what else her mother could do. If only *Betony* could make plants grow with magic.

"It's wonderful!" she said.

"Aye," Rosie said with satisfaction to the queen. "Green and growing, sweet and springlike, that's what you needed."

Indeed, Betony could see that her mother was looking much healthier than normal. Less pale and sad.

"What?" a booming voice said. "What *is* this?"

Betony knew that voice. It was the Lord Chancellor, the person who ran the country for her father, King Max. He sounded very cross.

Sure enough, there he was, standing at the doorway behind her father, who was looking at the growing green room with delight.

The Lord Chancellor, a stout man with a red face, was sputtering and spluttering and mopping his bald head with a spotted handkerchief.

It was, Betony realised, much warmer here than in the rest of the palace.

"It's unheard of," the chancellor said loudly. "Unheard of! Unacceptable! *Unqueenly*!" As though he'd already won the argument, whatever it was, he turned to the king and said, "It'll all have to go."

"There's no need to be hasty," her father began in his best "let's all get along" voice, but Rosie cut in, speaking as though the chancellor were a fairly stupid child.

"It's the queen's chamber, now and always. No sense fussing over it."

"It's got to go!" the chancellor declared. He kept sneaking glances at the walls, which were growing greener and leafier each moment. It was as if he were afraid of the plants. Which was silly, Betony thought, because any plants under Rosie's control were always well behaved. Even weeds didn't dare to seed themselves in her garden beds.

"It's spring," her mother said, her soft voice seeming to blend with the rustling of sprouting leaves. "I need green living things around me, or I will wilt away. I have been gone from the Wild Magic too long. I must bring some of it here to live with me, or my health will suffer."

Mention of the Wild Magic seemed to scare the Lord Chancellor so much that Betony didn't think he even heard the rest of what her mother had said.

"It's got to *go*," the chancellor shouted.

"It will not!" Her mother's voice had lost its softness. It was as sharp as an arrow made from willow wood, and as hard. "Lord Chancellor, this is where I draw the line. I have let you deprive my daughter of her heritage, I have let you cage me in this prison of stone, I have laboured hard to be a good and useful queen. But if these plants go, then I do too, back to the Forest where I belong."

"No!" Betony said.

Everyone looked at her and Lady Pineal came up from behind. "Let's leave your parents to discuss this, your Royal High—"

"You *can't* go." Betony hugged her mother tight. Salixia's strong arms came around her and held her close. "You belong with us." Betony reached out and pulled her father into the hug. For a moment it was wonderful – the three of them, together, as it should be.

Then the Lord Chancellor said sternly, "Your Royal Highness is interrupting a serious discussion. These are not manners which befit a princess."

Her father let go, and her mother turned Betony around in her arms so that she was facing the Lord Chancellor.

"Now, Lord Chancellor, I don't think—" her father said, but Betony was too angry and afraid to let him finish. What if her mother really did go away?

"This is all *your* fault," Betony shouted at the chancellor. "You're the one who is always being mean to my mother. You leave her alone! If she needs to have a forest in her room, she should have a forest. You are just … just … horrible and *stupid*."

A tendril of vine curled out from the wall and stroked Betony's face as though in approval. She could smell honeysuckle. Her mother's arms tightened for just a moment, as if she appreciated Betony sticking up for her.

"Betony!" her father said, and she knew she'd gone too far. It was his kinging voice, and he only used it when he was very annoyed. "That is enough."

"More than enough," the Lord Chancellor said. "I really do think, Your Majesty, that—"

"That the princess fights for those she loves, brave and honest," Rosie said quietly. "As a queen should be, always."

There was silence for a moment. Betony felt the warmth of Rosie's words bloom inside her chest, but she still felt angry. And scared.

"Go to your room," her father said, but this time it was his fathering voice, not his kinging voice. "But first, apologise to the Lord Chancellor."

Betony bit her lip. She couldn't. She just *couldn't.* The Lord Chancellor made her life horrible, but she'd never realised before that he made her mother's life horrible too.

"No," she said in a very small voice. "I can't."

"Then you will stay in your room until you can," Lady Pineal announced, taking her by the arm and pulling her away. "Until you understand the behaviour expected of a crown princess." She kept talking all the way to Betony's room and for a long time after that, but Betony hardly heard her. She was trying too hard to hear what was happening in her mother's chamber. What if the Lord Chancellor won? What if the plants were banished to the gardens?

Would her mother really go back to the Forest?

Back to the Dark Forest of Nevermore?

⊰ CHAPTER THREE ⊱

Betony was stuck in her room all morning and would have been there all day if she hadn't been allowed to go to her lesson with Rosie.

Rosemary Cecily Marigold Angelica Primrose Lavender was the Chief Palace Gardener and, for some reason Betony had never understood, was also one of her godmothers. She'd thought for quite a long time that Rosie was a *fairy* godmother, because she always seemed to know what Betony was thinking, but her mother had laughed at that.

"No, she's just a gardener," the queen had said. "Isn't that enough?"

Lady Pineal wasn't happy about letting Betony out, or about Betony's gardening clothes. "Overalls and gumboots are not suitable for a princess," she said. "Come straight back afterwards and change back into proper clothes."

Betony slid between the elm and oak trees that ringed the palace, out into the wider gardens.

She was never sure where she would find Rosie. The palace gardens were huge. There was a kitchen garden, that grew vegetables and soft fruit like strawberries; a herb garden; an orchard; a palmery in a little valley, where strange spiky plants sent striped shadows over the ground; a croquet lawn; a pleasure garden, where the courtiers promenaded and showed off their fine clothes; a grotto with its very own stream murmuring behind it; a small lake with swans; and a greenhouse, where Rosie grew exotic flowers and winter vegetables.

The palace gardens were safe and sound.

But at the end of the gardens, past where the stream chuckled and laughed, past a stand of silver birch trees which glowed gold in the sunset, was the Hill, and beyond it, the Dark Forest of Nevermore, which was the home of the Wild Magic. The Forest her mother might run away to.

Betony, of course, wasn't allowed anywhere near there. But she lingered, watching the shadows begin to fall across the Hill.

"Escaping, Bet?"

It was Rosie, seeming to appear out of nowhere, as she often did. She was an ordinary-looking woman in unimportant clothes, and she looked at Betony with shrewd eyes.

"Um ..." Betony answered.

"Hungry?" Rosie asked.

Lady Pineal didn't think rude little girls should have afternoon tea. Betony nodded.

"Come on then," the Chief Palace Gardener ordered.

They went to Rosie's own small cottage, which was tucked away between the green-house and the orchard, and was covered with untidy but beautiful vines: jasmine and passionfruit, grape and wisteria, all jumbled together in a maze of scent and greenery.

Betony followed Rosie inside to a kitchen with an old table in the middle. At the table sat a wizard.

Betony knew he was a wizard by the gleam in his eye and the fact that the book he was reading was floating in midair.

"This is Ralph," Rosie said. "Ralph, the princess. Sit you down, get you fed."

Obediently, Betony sat down and was given fresh tomato and dill soup, home-baked brown bread, and orange juice from Rosie's own orange trees. It was delicious, so Betony ate it all, and Rosie gave her a second helping of soup.

Betony looked out the window at the sunset sky to give herself courage, and then asked, "Rosie … why does my father let the Lord Chancellor boss my mother around?"

"Ah, well," Rosie answered slowly, as though she were thinking a problem through. "I'm not sure it's for me to say."

"I need to know," Betony cried.

Rosie looked deep into her eyes, and nodded decisively.

"So you do," she said. "It's because they're afraid of dragons."

⊰ CHAPTER FOUR ⊱

"What's a dragon?" Betony asked.

Ralph the Wizard waved his hand so that the big book floated gently down to the table. "What are they teaching you in that palace?" he exclaimed, surprised at her question.

"Nothing worth knowing," Rosie said grimly. "Show her, Ralph."

"Look into your soup, Your Highness," Ralph said. There was still a bit of bright red soup at the bottom of her bowl, so Betony looked. The soup went dark, and a picture appeared. A long, sinuous creature with wings and a curvy, spiky tail – blue and silver, like the sky with clouds. It flew with barely a movement of its wide, delicate wings. Beautiful like a hawk. The picture made Betony shiver.

"Aye, pretty and perilous, dragons," Rosie said. "They can steal the soul from a human with just a look. And that one was your mother's best friend before she married your father."

Betony looked up, astonished. It was one thing to know that her mother had once been the spirit of a tree, but somehow this was different – to be friends with a creature like that … that was truly not human. Betony understood for the first time that the Lord Chancellor and all the Royal Council were *afraid* of her mother.

Betony felt she could see the world in a whole new way. If her own mother could be friends with a creature like a dragon, anything was possible.

"No room in your head for gardening today," Rosie said. "We'll skip the lesson, I'm thinking. Or maybe it had better be a lesson about magic."

Betony almost said, "I'm not allowed to learn magic." She bit back the words. If she was going to understand her mother better, she had to learn, no matter what the Lord Chancellor said. But she couldn't help feeling a little scared. All her life she'd been told that the Wild Magic was dangerous. What if that were true?

Ralph smiled at her reassuringly.

"There is Human Magic," he said, "like I do." He waved his hand in the air and suddenly there was a rainbow, dancing on the end of his fingertips. He blew on it and it floated away, out the window. "And there is the Wild Magic, the magic of all living things. The Wild Magic cannot be tamed, cannot be controlled. It lives in the forests and the oceans, the mountains and the heaths, the wild places where humans do not go. Even humans have a bit of it, but not much. Not like hobgoblins, or pixies, or–"

"Fairies?" Betony asked eagerly.

Rosie chuckled and Ralph shook his head, smiling. "No fairies in Floramonde, I'm afraid. They don't get on with the dryads. But there are dwarves and dragons, trolls and giants, undines and naiads, griffins and rocs."

She'd never heard of any of those. She had so much to learn. Ralph winked at her and went to the window.

"Even ordinary animals can be magic," he said.

He whistled a complicated little tune with notes that didn't quite seem to fit. And down from the sky came a swallow, which swooped through the window and circled the room once, twice, three times before it flew out again, its wings flicking and dancing on the air.

Ralph whistled again, a different tune, and this time it was a robin that hopped up onto the window ledge and chirped a question at him.

"Come here, dryad's daughter," Ralph said. Slowly, Betony stood up and went to the window, waiting for the robin to take fright and fly away. But the little red-breasted bird stayed and looked at her with a bright, friendly eye.

"Put your hand out," Ralph said. Betony did, holding her breath. The robin jumped up onto her hand and perched there, the tiny claws holding her tightly.

"He likes you," Ralph said. "Maybe he can see your mother in you. Birds love the willow tree."

The robin chirped again as if in agreement and then, with a quick flirt of his tail, he turned around and flew out the window.

In a dream, Betony sat back down at the table. If only she could learn to call birds and animals like that! If only the Royal Council would let her learn magic.

"It's not all pretty," Ralph cautioned her. "There are other things too. Goblins, stone-eaters, harpies and hellhounds. The Wild Magic is not safe, Your Highness. It can be beautiful, but it is not safe – especially for humans."

That reminded Betony of the fear on the Lord Chancellor's face, and her own fear that her mother would go back to the Dark Forest.

"Do you think my mother will leave?" Betony asked.

"Your mother loves you," Rosie said. "Love finds its own road."

Betony wasn't sure if that was what she had wanted to hear, but it made her feel a bit better. They finished their food in silence, and then Rosie said, "They'll be looking for you."

Ralph waved his hand and muttered under his breath and said, "No, they won't. They'll be looking for a dog."

Not quite understanding, Betony said thank you and walked up the path to the palace.

When Betony went in the side door, the guards were off in a nearby room chasing a stray dog out of the palace. She laughed. *That* was what Ralph had meant.

She made her way back to her room. Lady Pineal wasn't there. Betony picked up her embroidery and started sewing before her governess arrived. She thought about dragons and goblins and – what *were* stone-eaters? Or hellhounds? She shivered as she sewed. They didn't sound very nice. On the other hand, the robin had been so sweet.

When Lady Pineal finally appeared, she was flustered and pink, muttering about mongrels and lax guards and falling standards. "We need a wizard around here," Lady Pineal finished, and Betony, thinking of Ralph, agreed with her.

Betony's roses were so badly sewn that Lady Pineal made her unpick them and do them again. She did it all in a daze, wondering what was happening in her mother's chamber, desperately hoping that her father had stopped the Lord Chancellor. That her mother was safe at home in her new green and living chamber.

She hoped to see one of her parents before bedtime to find out what had happened, but they were getting ready for a state dinner with the ambassador from Serendipity. She had her meal with Lady Pineal in the smallest dining room instead, and was chivvied off to bed without even saying goodnight to her parents.

"You know they don't have time tonight," Lady Pineal scolded. "Don't be unreasonable."

Frustrated – and still feeling very churned up inside – Betony got ready for bed, while Lady Pineal closed all the windows tightly, for fear of the night air.

Betony had trouble sleeping, her thoughts were whirling around so fast, and she woke earlier than ever before, when the sky was still almost all black, and the stars had just begun to fade.

She went to the window and opened it wide, breathing in the fresh, still night air. Below her, a door opened and someone came out onto the terrace.

A woman. She was just a shadow, but something in the way she moved made Betony sure it was her mother.

"Mother," she hissed, but her mother didn't hear. The shadowy figure set out across the terrace and down to the lawn below, heading across the grounds.

Betony's breath caught in her throat.

Her mother was going into the Dark Forest of Nevermore. She was leaving.

↠ CHAPTER FIVE ↞

Betony scrambled out of her nightgown and back into her gardening clothes as fast as she could. She gulped back tears. She had to stop her mother leaving! And if she couldn't stop her, then she'd just have to go too, she decided, and live in the Forest.

She tiptoed past Lady Pineal's room, holding her breath, and down the back stairs to the side hall. Every ten minutes or so, the palace guards marched back and forth along the hall. She crouched behind a statue of her great-grandfather, King Mortimer the Very Fat, and waited, her heart beating fast. The guards turned and saluted each other and while their hands were over their eyes, Betony crept past them into the great shadowy kitchen.

The fire smouldered gently in the huge grate, banked down for the night. The kitchen smelled of honey and bacon and smoke, and Betony seemed to hear whispers from the rafters where the hams

and sausages hung. Was it ghosts or mice? Bats or poltergeists?

Right at the back of the kitchen was a small window that was always left open for the kitchen cat. Betony walked as quietly as she could towards it. Then, from a side room, came a bang and a thump and several voices.

"Fifteen loaves at least," one said.

Of course. The palace bakers started work halfway through the night, to make the fresh bread for breakfast. Betony stood frozen for a moment. The door to the

baker's workroom began to open slowly. Should she run back to her bedroom? Betony wanted to, but she wanted to stop her mother even more.

So she ran, helter-skelter, skimble-skamble, fast as she could to the little window. The baker's door was opening. She had to move quickly.

She began to climb the table that stood under the window. She risked a look back as she hauled herself up to the window. A boy stood there, holding a tray of bread rolls, silhouetted against the light so she couldn't see his face. He took in a breath as he saw her, as if he was going to call out, but then he stepped back into the bakery and called back over his shoulder, "How many loaves did you say, Da?"

Betony got her foot hooked onto the windowsill and levered herself up. She looked back and waved a thank you to the baker's boy. He nodded. Then she was

through and out. It was a long drop to the ground, but the grass was soft and she fell with no more than the breath knocked out of her.

There was a bush between her and the guards outside the side door, and a patch of thistles behind her. Ignoring the prickles, she pushed through and then ran and ran across the garden, grass brushing cold dew on her bare legs, the sky showing grey

above the trees, up over the top of the Hill, where she had never gone before, until the Forest lay in front of her, black and huge and menacing.

Betony stood at the bottom of the other side of the Hill, her toes in the stream which separated the palace grounds from the Forest. All her life she had heard whispered stories about how dangerous the Forest was. It was the home of the Wild Magic.

She thought about goblins and wolves and giants.

Her heart beat like the guards' drums at marching practice. So hard she could almost hear it. She was frightened.

But she had to stop her mother. If her mother left them, she might never return. The Wild Magic might not let her. Or … or maybe she would turn herself back into a willow tree, and then she wouldn't be *able* to come back.

She would be rooted somewhere out in the Dark Forest, alone and far away. And Betony was sure that the Royal Council wouldn't let her visit her mother if that happened. She might never see Salixia again.

Betony took a deep breath, leaped over the stream and ran into the tall fir trees, which marked the edge of the Forest.

Under the trees it was dark and smelled sharply of pine. The trunks of the trees were patched with orange lichen, and the trees rustled high above her head. They sounded … sneaky.

Don't be silly, Betony told herself. Trees can't be sneaky.

But how much did she really know about trees?

She wished her father were with her.

With the firs hissing in the wind, Betony was sure that if these trees had dryad spirits, they wouldn't be very nice. She could feel a slow prickle along her skin, as though there was something trying to get inside her. Was that the Wild Magic?

Betony wanted to go home. But her mother was out there, somewhere, in the dark woods. She had to go deeper.

⊰ CHAPTER SIX ⊱

The wind whispered to her, and Betony felt that she could almost understand it. It seemed to blow more strongly on her left side, as if it wanted to push her to the right, and since she didn't have any other way of deciding where to go, she let it guide her.

Underneath the whisper was another sound, of water flowing over rocks. Willow trees liked water, didn't they? Perhaps her mother had come this way.

The dark trunks of the trees blocked her view, but then she moved around one huge old pine and found a clearing, with a pool in the centre of it, fed by a little stream. And there, on the other side of the pool, outlined in the faint light, were two beings … a horsey shape with a long pearly horn in its forehead, and a green-clad woman, who placed a hand on the horse-thing's neck. For a moment, Betony thought it was her mother, but this woman was taller and had much darker hair.

The horse-thing was as pure white as snow or summer cloud. Even in this pale early light, its horn spiralled up in glinting gleams of every colour, like the mother-of-pearl buttons on Betony's best ball dress. When it moved its feet it seemed to dance.

The woman danced too. She raised her arms high like tree branches, and swayed and curved with the wind, with the trees around her, with the horse-thing, as it dipped its horn and picked up its feet

so delicately it appeared to float. It was the most beautiful thing Betony had ever seen.

She wished that Ralph had taught her more about the magical creatures of Floramonde – she would love to know what this beautiful creature was called.

Her heart tightened. She wanted so much to join that dance, to float above the moss-green forest floor, to dip and bow in time with that glowing horn. But the dance was so clearly a thing of magic, and she was just human. The prickle on her skin was now so strong it almost hurt. She felt as though she were hungry, watching other people eat and knowing there would be no food for her.

She sighed.

At once, the wind died.

The green-clad woman turned and the horse-thing lowered its horn and snorted. They both looked at her. Betony felt embarrassed and a bit scared. Now that it was pointed at her, the horn looked very sharp.

"Name yourself," the woman said, in a voice that sounded like the breeze in the pine trees. Her face was sharp and her dark brown hair spiky. It was not a nice face, although it wasn't nasty either. But she looked at Betony with sternness, as though she had the right to judge her.

"I'm Betony. Princess Betony."

"The willow tree's daughter," the woman said. Her voice was thoughtful, but not welcoming.

"I'm looking for my mother," Betony said.

"She is in the Forest, indeed," the woman said, "but you may not search here unless you can prove yourself one of us. The Forest is forbidden to humans, and will destroy you unless your heart belongs to the Wild Magic."

The Wild Magic!

But Betony was human. She had never seen any sign that she was anything else. No magic. Nothing – except the robin which had come to her hand.

"How can I be a part of the Wild Magic if I'm human?" she asked. Deep in her heart she *wanted* to be part of it. Wanted to be strange and magical. The horse-thing snickered as though she had said something funny.

"*Are* you human? Are you *all* human? Or are you truly your mother's daughter?" the woman asked. "Your mother was a dryad, a tree spirit, as I am. But what are you?"

Hope began to bloom in Betony's chest. Could she be something magical? Was that possible? The wind began to sing again as if in answer.

"That is what you must find out," the dryad said. Betony was suddenly sure that the dryad was the spirit of a pine tree, spiky and sharp-natured. "If you pass the test and show us that you are part of the Wild Magic, the Forest will let you search for your mother, and you may take her back to your prison of a palace. But if you don't … if you are truly *all* human …" The pine-tree spirit looked deep into the horse-thing's eyes. "You may not search for her without great peril."

Betony's heart clenched and her stomach grew heavy, but she lifted her chin. She would get her mother back. She would!

"What test?"

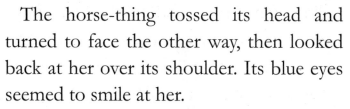

The horse-thing tossed its head and turned to face the other way, then looked back at her over its shoulder. Its blue eyes seemed to smile at her.

"Catch the unicorn," the dryad said. "Only a creature whose heart belongs to the Wild Magic can catch a unicorn."

The horse-thing was a unicorn! Even Betony had heard of them. They were the heart of the Wild Magic. Very rare. Very special.

The wind rose and seemed to push Betony in the small of her back again. She took a step forwards and immediately the unicorn sprang away, galloping towards the darkness of the trees.

"Run," the dryad commanded.

"I won't be able to catch that."

"If you are wild enough, the Forest will help you. But if you do not try, you may never find your mother. Salixia still belongs here and the Forest protects its own from humans." Betony couldn't tell if the dryad was sympathetic or nasty.

"Run!"

So Betony ran, her heart lifting with hope, even though her head was full of confusion.

⊰ CHAPTER SEVEN ⊱

Betony chased the unicorn's hoofbeats through the pine trees. They were always just too far ahead, but every so often she would see a white tail flick around a tree trunk, or catch a glimpse of a shining horn. She tried her best to run fast, but princesses are not allowed to run much, so she got out of breath quickly.

She stopped for a moment, panting, her hands on her knees, and realised that she was not in the pine trees any more.

This was beech forest, with old leaves from hundreds of years of autumns carpeting the ground, and the bright green of spring leaves whispering above her.

The beech trees had bigger gaps between them than the pine trees, so she could see further ahead, but she couldn't see the unicorn anywhere. The wind died. The forest was still.

Yet she could not hear the unicorn's hooves.

Betony had no idea where she was. Her heart began thudding even harder than it had while she was running.

"Think," she told herself. "This must be part of the test."

She couldn't think of what to do next, except to give up.

The palace had to be west of the Forest. So when the sun was finally up, she could just keep its rays on her back and she would find her way out. Her heart slowed a little. She could go home.

But she wasn't going home without her mother. For a moment, she wondered what she would do if she found her mother and Salixia just didn't want to come home with her. Fear and sadness curled her stomach tight, and her palms were wet with sweat just thinking about it.

Lady Pineal often said to Betony, "You

are so stubborn, Your Highness!" and this was supposed to be a bad thing in a princess. But now Betony was glad of every bit of stubbornness in her. She was not giving up.

Rosie often said, "Too stubborn to give up, that's good. Too stubborn to ask for help, that's stupid."

So Betony, the dryad's daughter, cleared her throat and spoke to the beech trees with her best princess manners.

"Most honoured beeches, if there be a dryad amongst you, may I have speech of you?"

A rustle went through the trees, although there was no wind. Then, one by one, heads emerged from the beech trees, sticking out of the wood as you might stick your head through an open window.

It was a very strange sight. Betony's stomach turned a little, to see pretty girls' faces seeming to be stuck onto the tree trunks.

The faces were full of curiosity. Eyes inspected her. Mouths pursed, or half-smiled, or were set straight. Then they all stepped out of their trees as you might step from behind a slit in a curtain.

They looked very much alike, these dryads, but they were not identical any more than two beech trees are identical. Their hair was russet-

brown, glinting red, and their eyes were the deep green of beech leaves in summer, but some were tall and some were short, some were slender and others quite stout.

They surrounded Betony. She counted eighteen of them before the one closest to her spoke.

"You are not tree, but you have the scent of tree about you. What are you?"

"A willow tree's daughter," Betony said. She was pretty sure that being a princess didn't count for much here.

"Ahh," they said in unison, like trees sighing together in the wind.

"I'm looking for my mother, but I have to catch the unicorn first or the Forest won't let me find her."

Tears pricked Betony's eyes. It seemed so hopeless. But she couldn't give up.

The dryads laughed, and their trees seemed to laugh with them, rustling their branches and leaves.

"You will not find the unicorn. The unicorn finds you when you are fleet of foot and light of heart. Come. Run and laugh!"

They snatched at Betony's hands and urged her to run, faster than she had done before.

With her hands in theirs she felt as though she could run forever. As though the sun, which was just peering over the horizon, was flooding her with strength.

When the dryads laughed with the delight of morning, Betony laughed too. They jumped over fallen logs, and she jumped with them. She was full of joy so great it almost pushed out the deep fear that she would never find her mother.

⊰ CHAPTER EIGHT ⊱

They came to the edge of the beech wood, to where pines began again, and the dryads stopped.

"Go on," they said, their voices fluting like birds. "Run and laugh."

Betony waved to them and kept on running. She could hear woodpeckers tapping a rhythm high above and her feet fell into time with the noise. The tall trees no longer seemed sneaky and strange – in the warming light they seemed like friendly ladies in waiting, spreading their green skirts to the air. As the dryads had, Betony

leaped high over fallen saplings, and
across streams that chuckled over rounded
pebbles.

She laughed, and the wind seemed to
laugh with her. She imagined finding
the unicorn. She couldn't quite imagine
dancing with it, but perhaps it would let
her ride it through the Forest, trotting
elegantly through the trees. How lovely
that would be. Then they would find her
mother together …

She heard hoofbeats ahead of her, and she quickened her pace. But although she raced as fast as she could, she couldn't see the unicorn.

Without the dryads to help her along, her feet were beginning to hurt. She'd never run so far before. Panting a little, she stopped to drink from one of the little streams. On the other side of the stream was an actual path, a clear track which led from left to right. One way led deeper into the Forest.

The other led west, back towards the palace.

She had run and looked and run and laughed, but there was no sign of the unicorn, or of her mother. The sun was coming up. If she couldn't find Salixia, should she go back to the palace and ask Ralph for help?

Now she had stopped running, all the gaiety had drained out of her.

She was discouraged and tired and hungry. Looking down the path which led deeper into the Forest, she was also a bit nervous.

A horse neighed somewhere in the shadows; it sounded frightened. Betony hesitated for just a heartbeat. The unicorn! It was frightened. She shivered at the thought of the things lurking in this Forest that could frighten a unicorn, armed as it was with its long horn. She wanted to run back to the palace and lock the door behind her. All the stories she had ever heard whispered about the Forest came flooding into her mind, and she felt her stomach cramp with fear.

Then the unicorn squealed again and Betony's feet took off without her even thinking.

The path twisted and dipped down almost straightaway, leading her into a valley filled with alder and oak saplings struggling up through brambles and briars, which caught at her clothes and her hair, snatching at her hands with sharp thorns. It was darker here, and the wind was louder. Ahead of her, she could hear a wild thrashing, as though a giant was tossing and turning on a bed of trees.

She gulped, but she kept running on, as though her feet didn't know how to stop, even though her mind was racing, imagining monsters or giants or who knew what attacking the unicorn, and not knowing what she could do about any of them.

At the bottom of the valley she came to a tumbling brook, wider than the other streams she had crossed. With legs flailing, Betony jumped, willing herself across.

She stumbled as she landed, and she almost fell backwards into the water, but she flapped her arms and leaned forwards and managed to stay upright, staggering through the bushes on the other side of the brook into a clearing beyond.

Right in front of her, in the middle of the clearing, was the unicorn.

Its horn was down, holding back a huge black wolf which snarled at it, the growl rising and falling in the suddenly still air.

That noise made all the hair on Betony's neck stand up and her stomach seemed to rise into her throat. Her knees shook.

There was a long claw mark on the unicorn's white side and blood dripped out.

The wolf leaped. With a flick of its horn, the unicorn slammed it aside and Betony felt a surge of relief. It didn't need her help. She didn't have to do anything. But then the wolf rolled and came to its feet in one smooth move and attacked again, launching itself at the unicorn's throat.

The unicorn reared and neighed – the high, terrified trumpet she had heard earlier. It flailed at the wolf with its hooves. It was getting tired, its flanks spotted with sweat and blood.

Betony looked around frantically. Surely there would be someone who could help?

What could *she* do? She was a princess, not a soldier or a hunter.

There was no one else. The wolf crouched, ready to attack again. Betony could hear the unicorn's heavy panting. It sounded so tired.

She grabbed a branch from the ground and ran forwards, shouting as loudly as she could.

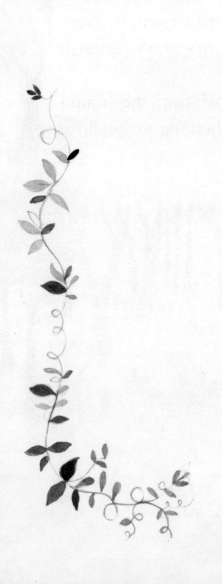

⊰ CHAPTER NINE ⊱

The wolf spun to face her. It snarled, and crouched as if to spring at her. Betony didn't wait for it to move. She ran straight at it, bringing the branch down as hard as she could. It dodged, but she hit it on the back and it yelped with pain.

Betony brought the branch up again and, from the corner of her eye, saw the unicorn turn as if it was going to run for the safety of the Forest. Half of her wanted it to, wanted it to get to cover – but the other half almost screamed with panic.

The wolf sprang at Betony's throat, its

body seeming to lengthen as it leaped into the air. For a long moment, it blocked out the light as it arced towards her. It looked twice as big as it had on the ground, and Betony couldn't make herself move. She began to swing the branch, but the wolf was moving so fast, she knew it wouldn't connect in time.

Then the unicorn kicked backwards with both hind feet and the wolf tumbled out of the air and onto the ground, its breath slammed out of its body. It lay there, shuddering, and then it dragged itself up and glared at them both, blood and spit sliding from the corner of its mouth.

There was red hatred in that look, and it made Betony feel sick. Next to her, the unicorn's warm shoulder helped her to stand tall. She raised the branch again and stared the wolf straight in the eyes.

With a snarl, the wolf limped away into the shadows of the pines and the clearing was peaceful once more.

Slowly,
Betony
dropped the
branch and turned to face
the unicorn, who bowed its head to
her, pawing the grass with one hoof.

Then it threw up its head and neighed, a triumphant blare that lifted Betony's spirits up into the sky.

As the unicorn stood there, head high, the sun slipped over the tall trees and caught the unicorn's pearly horn in a blaze of light, as though the moon was shining brightly in the clearing to challenge the sun.

Betony was filled with a wild joy, with an explosion of happiness so that she felt she could jump straight up to the top of the birch trees, and maybe past that and on to the stars.

She wanted to sing; she wanted to shout; she wanted to cry. But instead she put her hand out very carefully, touched the

unicorn's warm cheek, and stroked it.

Then she put her arm around its neck and hugged it, and it didn't seem to mind because it whickered softly, as if it were laughing.

There was a pool nearby. They drank the clear water together. The water seemed to take all her tiredness away and afterwards she

saw that the wound on the unicorn's side had closed and healed as if it had never been.

Betony stared into the unicorn's beautiful blue eyes and loved it with all her heart. She wanted to stay with it forever.

But surely there was something she should be doing?

For a moment, she felt confused. Why was she here? What was she doing in the Forest? She couldn't remember. It seemed to her that nothing was more important than being with the unicorn, but there was a feeling at the back of her mind that she had forgotten something.

Betony pulled her gaze away from the unicorn's eyes and, with a rush, she remembered everything. Her heart beat faster and her breath came short. How could she have forgotten her mother? The Wild Magic *was* dangerous, although not in the way she had thought. It could steal your heart and your mind and enchant you away from your real life. But she wouldn't let that happen. Not to her, and not to her mother.

"Do you know where my mother is, unicorn?" she asked.

The unicorn nosed her cheek, stroked her side with its shining horn, and galloped silently away. Betony didn't run after it, but she followed the path it had taken, and there, at the end of the path, was a small clearing with a grove of willow trees.

On one of the low willow branches, a woman in green sat and talked quietly to the unicorn. The unicorn turned its head towards her and seemed to smile, then it slid away behind the willow trees and was gone.

The woman was her mother.

❧ CHAPTER TEN ❧

*S*alixia smiled at Betony and held out her arms. Betony walked into them and felt the strong, warm hands hold her tightly. She sighed happily, and snuggled in.

"So you have fought a wolf and defended a unicorn," her mother said.

"How did you know?"

Salixia laughed. "The wind told me, just now," she said.

The wind? Who could understand the wind? The trees? There was so much to learn, but the most important thing was to convince her mother to come back. Fighting the wolf seemed easy in comparison.

"Please don't leave us," she said.

The laughter stilled in Salixia's eyes, and was replaced by astonishment.

"I wasn't going to," she said. She slid her arm around Betony's shoulders and hugged her tight. "I often come to the Forest in the early morning."

"But the dryad said ... and the Lord Chancellor. Your chamber–" Betony was so tired that she could scarcely speak straight.

"Your father has informed the Lord Chancellor that he has no power over the queen," her mother said. "Your father would never let the Royal Council do anything that would harm either of us. And I need those plants, to be healthy."

Betony was silent for a moment, thoughts and feelings rolling around in her so fast she felt dizzy. One thing was clearest in her mind. Her mother had always meant to come home.

"So I didn't even need to be tested?" she asked. It felt like she'd been cheated, or tricked.

"Well," her mother said slowly, "it's true that I would have come back – but that wasn't what you asked the Forest, was it? You asked to find me. And you would not have found me without passing the test."

She got up and dusted down her skirt. "You have gained a great deal, you know. Not only do you have the freedom of the Forest, but you know now that you are truly part of the Wild Magic. Someone fully human would not have been able to look away from the unicorn's eyes. They would have stared until the unicorn itself moved away. That was the second part of the test."

That was almost too much to take in. Betony wondered if maybe she could do magic too, like Ralph or her mother. Make plants grow, or call robins to her.

"I need to know about Wild Magic," she said finally.

"Yes, you do. You are the heir to Floramonde, and one day you will be queen," her mother said as they began to walk back to the palace. "But you inherit a different realm through me – the realm of Wild Magic." She smiled, her eyes seeming to reflect the whole green world. "There'll be time to talk about all that. But now you have won acceptance from the Forest, you can come here too."

Betony looked around her with new eyes.

The Forest was still unpredictable, but not as scary as before. She would come back.

"We'd better get home before your father gets too worried," her mother said. "Just remember, I love you, and I would never leave you."

With the unicorn Betony had felt triumph and joy. But this was better. Much better. And it was all she really needed to know.

At the palace they found everyone running here and there, organising search parties to go and look for them – except Rosie, who was quietly watering the flowers on the terrace. She smiled at Betony as if she already knew everything that Betony had done.

Inside, Betony's father was on his throne, talking to the Lord Chancellor and Ralph, loudly, about trying a locating spell to find them. The Lord Chancellor didn't seem happy.

Betony walked right into the throne room, her mother behind her. She looked around at all the bustling courtiers and asked, "What does a person have to do to get some breakfast around here?"

Her mother laughed. Her father leaped off the throne and hugged Betony hard. Lady Pineal squealed in indignation and used her worst scolding voice.

"Princess Betony," she said, very high and mighty.

"How *could* you? How dare you! Do you realise what you have done?"

Betony really couldn't be bothered with all of that. She was her mother's daughter, after all, *not* Lady Pineal's. She pulled back from her father and turned to face her governess.

"My mother's friends knew where I was, Lady Pineal," she said, polite but firm. "So there was no need for anyone to be alarmed."

Rosie laughed, and Lady Pineal glared at her, but her father nodded. He slung an arm around Betony's shoulders.

"Quite right," he said.

"Betony has won acceptance from the Dark Forest of Nevermore," her mother said.

There was a shocked silence.

"Really?" her father said slowly. "Hmm."

"I need to learn more about the Wild Magic, Dad," Betony said. "I won't be able to be a good queen in Floramonde if I don't know about it." She crossed her fingers.

"You need to know about Human Magic too," he agreed. Betony jumped with excitement.

The Lord Chancellor, Lady Pineal and half-a-dozen other courtiers tried to protest, but the king waved them to silence.

"And the person best suited to this task is our new Court Wizard, Ralph … er, do you have another name?" he asked Ralph. "Ralph the Mighty, or Ralph the Wise, or something like that?"

"Just Ralph," the new Court Wizard said, smiling. "We will start lessons about unicorns and dragons in the morning."

Betony jiggled on her toes with satisfaction and excitement until her father hugged her tight to keep her still. Her mother came over to them and he pulled her into the hug. Betony closed her eyes and snuggled closer to both of her parents. It was the same as it had been the day before, just the three of them, but now there was nothing to spoil it.

Princess Betony buried her face against her mother's warm side and smiled secretly. Unicorns and dragons and the freedom of the Forest. From here on, she thought, *anything* could happen.

Princess Betony has been chosen to collect a gift from the Wild Magic – a precious thunder egg that has to be protected at all costs.

Betony must journey alone through the Dark Forest to Teapot Mountain and bring the egg back safely.

If not, the Wild Magic will seek revenge.

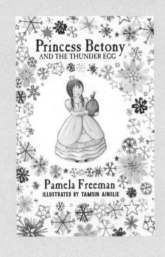

Princess Betony
AND THE RULE OF WISHING

Princess Betony is delighted to have found a proper friend at last – Rosie's niece, Clover Pink.

But having a friend isn't as easy as Betony first thought.

Especially when Clover decides she wants to become a witch and desperately needs to discover the Rule of Wishing.

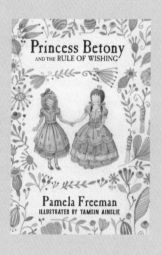

Princess Betony
AND THE HOBGOBLIN

The hobgoblin is not happy!
The kitchen staff have stopped
leaving milk out for him. And
an unhappy hobgoblin means
trouble!

Princess Betony is sure she can
win him over. But can she do
it before all the hobgoblins
attack?

To find out more about
Princess Betony and
Floramonde go to:
princessbetony.com